Little
Look and Find

DISNEP
MINNIE

Illustrated by Art Mawhinney

Published by
Louis Weber, C.E.O.
Publications International, Ltd.
7373 North Cicero Avenue
Lincolnwood, Illinois 60712

Lower Ground Floor, 59 Gloucester Place
London W1U 8JJ

Customer Service: 1-800-595-8484
or customer_service@pilbooks.com

www.pilbooks.com

p i kids is a trademark of Publications International, Ltd., and is registered in the United States.

Look and Find is a trademark of Publications International, Ltd., and is registered in the United States and Canada.

Little Look and Find is a trademark of Publications International, Ltd.

8 7 6 5 4 3 2 1

Manufactured in China.

ISBN: 978-1-4508-8336-8

Minnie is excited to have a day off. There's nothing more relaxing than sitting down with a good book. While Minnie browses the bookshelves for something to read, look for these friends who are also at the library:

Chip and Dale

Mickey

Donald

Daisy

Pluto

Uncle Scrooge

Goofy

STORY
TIME

Yummy! Minnie knows there's nothing like a sweet treat to help her relax. So she heads to the busy bakery, which is not very relaxing at all! While Minnie picks out a snack, look for each of these delicious desserts:

banana bread

red velvet cupcake

this cinnamon bun

chocolate chip cookie

strawberry pie

carrot cake

this donut

Some fresh flowers will brighten Minnie's day! She goes to the greenhouse to buy some. But it's *so* busy. Gardening things and green thumbs are everywhere! Help Minnie pick a nice bouquet by finding these pretty plants:

this cactus

lemon tree

Venus flytrap

daisy

peanut plant

bonsai tree

watermelon plant

wreath made of roses

tomato plant

SPECIAL

Oh, dear! Minnie's in the middle of a hectic parking lot, and her car has a flat tire! Luckily, she knows how to fix it herself. While Minnie works on her car, look for these other types of transportation all around her:

pogo stick

kite

scooter

roller skates

skateboard

bicycle

Now that her hands are all dirty from changing her tire, Minnie decides to get a manicure. The beauty salon is packed! While Minnie soaks her tired hands, look for these beauty-related things:

shaving cream

hair trimmer

cucumber slices

nail clippers

shampoo

hair dryer

Minnie is on her way home when she passes the Blue Ribbon Pet Show. Always a good friend, she stops to cheer for Pluto and Mickey. While Minnie roots for her pals, look for these other animals who want to win:

frog

goldfish

this kitten

hamster

macaw

this puppy

boa constrictor

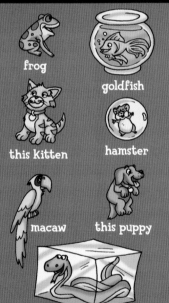

To congratulate Pluto for winning a blue ribbon, Minnie and Mickey take him for a walk in the park. But it's not a very calm way to end the day. Look for these crazy things that are going on:

At last,
Minnie's busy day is
done and it's time to relax.
But look! Minnie is too tired
to enjoy her book or flowers
or treat. She has fallen right
to sleep! While Minnie snoozes,
search for these things she
picked up during the day:

library book

this bouquet

nail polish

jack for her car

Pluto's blue
ribbon

cupcake

Go back to the
library and find these
storybook characters
hidden around the scene:

Humpty
Dumpty

Little Red
Riding Hood

Mother
Goose

Big Bad Wolf

Rumpelstiltskin

Emperor wearing
new clothes

Three Little
Pigs

Get back in line
at the bakery and look
for these baking ingredients:

milk

eggs

icing

chocolate
chips

flour

sugar

banana

Tiptoe through
the tulips until you get
to the greenhouse. Then
search for these things that
might help your garden grow:

watering
can

flowerpot

packet of
seeds

garden
hoe

bag of fertilizer

hose

Fertilizer

Pull back into
the parking lot and
look for these silly vehicles:

dogsled

clown car

Toon Car

ice-cream cart

Scrooge's fancy car

balloon cart

Donald's car in a
fender bender

Slip back into
the beauty salon and
seek out these stylish services:

- shampoo
- haircut
- massage
- pedicure
- shave
- mud mask

Scamper, soar,
swim, or slither back to
the Blue Ribbon Pet Show
and look for these pets
you don't see every day:

fox

timber wolf

stingray

Komodo dragon

dodo

beaver

Stroll back
through the park
and spot these more
normal outdoor items:

soccer
ball

golf club

bread for
feeding ducks

flying
disc

picnic
basket

foot bag

Quietly go
back to Minnie's house
to find 12 matching
pairs of plants: